The HELEN OXENBURY
Nursery Collection

The HELEN OXENBURY
Nursery Collection

To Huckleberry

THIS IS A BORZOI BOOK PUBLISHED BY ALFRED A. KNOPF
Stories and rhymes selected from:
Tiny Tim — Verses for Children © 1981 by Helen Oxenbury
Cakes and Custard — The Helen Oxenbury Nursery Rhyme Book © 1974, 1986 by Helen Oxenbury
The Helen Oxenbury Nursery Story Book © 1985 by Helen Oxenbury

KNOPF, BORZOI BOOKS, and the colophon are registered trademarks of Random House, Inc.
www.randomhouse.com/kids
Library of Congress Cataloging-in-Publication Data available upon request.
ISBN 0-375-82992-X (trade)
ISBN 0-375-92992-4 (lib. bdg.)
Acknowledgments:
The illustrator and publisher would like to thank the following for permission to reproduce the poems in this
book: The Society of Authors as the Literary Representative of the Estate of Rose Fyleman for "Mice";
Scholastic Limited for "Down Behind the Dustbin" from *Mind Your Own Business* copyright © 1974
by Michael Rosen, first published by André Deutsch Limited.

Manufactured in Italy
10 9 8 7 6 5 4 3 2 1
First American Edition
October 2004

The HELEN OXENBURY
Nursery Collection

ALFRED A. KNOPF   NEW YORK

CONTENTS

NURSERY STORIES

Nursery stories and rhymes
belong to children.
They can be anarchic, cruel
or comforting — helping
children to cope with the
playground and learn about
their world.
They stay with you all your life

Helen Oxenbury.

Verses from

TINY TIM

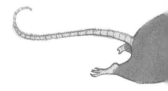

I THINK MICE
Are rather nice.
Their tails are long
Their faces small.
They haven't any chins at all.
Their ears are pink,
Their teeth are white,
They run about
The house at night.
They nibble things
They shouldn't touch
And no one seems
To like them much.
But I think mice
Are rather nice.

ROSE FYLEMAN

DOWN BEHIND THE DUSTBIN
I met a dog called Jim.
He didn't know me
And I didn't know him.

MICHAEL ROSEN

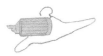

NEW SHOES, NEW SHOES,
Red and pink and blue shoes,
Tell me what would *you* choose
If they'd let us buy?

Buckle shoes, bow shoes,
Pretty pointy-toe shoes,
Strappy, cappy low shoes;
Let's have some to try.

Bright shoes, white shoes,
Dandy dance-by-night shoes,
Perhaps-a-little-tight shoes;
Like some? So would I.

BUT

Flat shoes, fat shoes,
Stump-along-like-that shoes,
Wipe-them-on-the-mat shoes
O that's the sort they'll buy.

FFRIDA WOLFE

I HAVE A LITTLE BROTHER
His name is Tiny Tim
I put him in the bathtub
To teach him how to swim
He drank up all the water
He ate up all the soap
Lay down on the bathmat
Blowing bubbles from his throat

In came the doctor
In came the nurse
In came the lady
With the alligator purse
NAUGHTY! said the doctor
WICKED! said the nurse
Wind said the lady
With the alligator purse
Out went the doctor
Out went the nurse
Out went the lady
With the alligator purse.

ANON

GRANDMA GURNEY
Gives to me
Gooseberry tart
And hot sweet tea.

She sits up high
On her rocking chair.
She can't touch the floor
But she doesn't care.

Grandma Gurney
Is tiny and gray.
I wonder if
She'll shrink away?

Grandma Gurney
Has grown very small.
One day she won't be
There at all.

A. E. DUDLEY

NURSERY
RHYMES

SING A SONG OF SIXPENCE,
A pocket full of rye;
Four and twenty blackbirds
Baked in a pie;

When the pie was opened
The birds began to sing;
Wasn't that a dainty dish
To set before the king?

The king was in his counting house
Counting out his money;
The queen was in the parlor
Eating bread and honey;

The maid was in the garden
Hanging out the clothes,
There came a little blackbird,
And snapped off her nose.

Jenny was so mad,
She didn't know what to do;
She put her finger in her ear,
And cracked it right in two.

BABY AND I
Were baked in a pie,
The gravy was wonderful hot;
We had nothing to pay
To the baker that day,
And so we crept out of the pot.

As I was going up Pippen Hill,
Pippen Hill was dirty,
There I met a pretty miss,
And she dropped me a curtsy.

Little miss, pretty miss,
Blessings light upon you!
If I had half-a-crown a day,
I'd spend it all upon you.

WHEN GOOD KING ARTHUR ruled this land,
He was a goodly king;
He stole three pecks of barley-meal,
To make a bag-pudding.

A bag-pudding the king did make,
And stuff'd it well with plums;
And in it put great lumps of fat,
As big as my two thumbs.

The king and queen did eat thereof,
And noblemen beside;
And what they could not eat that night,
The queen next morning fried.

Barber, barber, shave a pig,
How many hairs will make a wig?
"Four and twenty, that's enough,"
Give the barber a pinch of snuff.

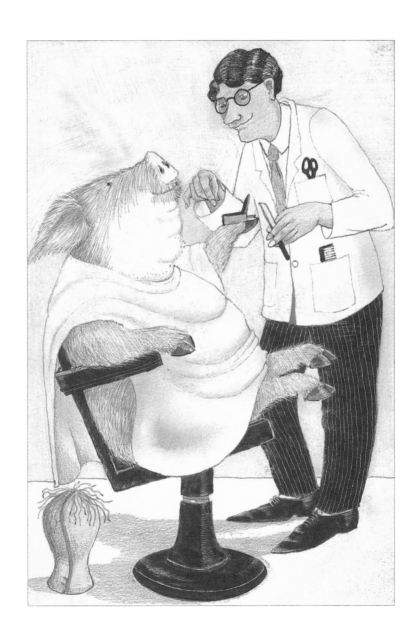

DESPERATE DAN
The dirty old man
Washed his face
In a frying pan;
Combed his hair
With the leg of a chair;
Desperate Dan
The dirty old man.

ON SATURDAY NIGHT
Shall be all my care,
To powder my locks
And curl my hair.

On Sunday morning
My love will come in,
When he will marry me
With a gold ring.

THERE WAS AN OLD WOMAN sat spinning,

And that's the first beginning;

She had a calf,

And that's half,

She took it by the tail,

And threw it over the wall,

And that's all.

ELSIE MARLEY is grown so fine,
  She won't get up to serve the swine,
But lies in bed till eight or nine,
And surely she does take her time.

And do you know Elsie Marley, honey?
The wife who sells the barley, honey;
She won't get up to serve her swine,
And do you know Elsie Marley, honey?

W HO COMES HERE?
   A grenadier.
What do you want?
   A pot of beer.
Where's your money?
   I've forgot.
Then get you gone
   You drunken sot!

LITTLE TOM TUCKER
Sings for his supper;
What shall he eat?
White bread and butter.
How shall he cut it
Without e'er a knife?
How will he be married
Without e'er a wife?

A MAN OF WORDS and not of deeds,
   Is like a garden full of weeds;
And when the weeds begin to grow,
   It's like a garden full of snow;
   And when the snow begins to fall,
   It's like a bird upon the wall;
   And when the bird away does fly,
   It's like an eagle in the sky;
   And when the sky begins to roar,
   It's like a lion at the door;
And when the door begins to crack,
It's like a stick across your back;
And when your back begins to smart,
It's like a penknife in your heart;
   And when your heart begins to bleed,
   You're dead, and dead, and dead indeed!

NURSERY STORIES

LITTLE RED RIDING HOOD

~

THERE WAS ONCE A LITTLE GIRL whose mother made her a new cloak with a hood. It was a lovely red color and she liked to wear it so much that everyone called her Little Red Riding Hood.

One day her mother said to her, "I want you to take this basket of cakes to your grandmother, who is ill."

Little Red Riding Hood liked to walk through the woods to her grandmother's cottage and she quickly put on her cloak. As she was leaving, her mother said, "Now remember, don't talk to any strangers on the way."

But Little Red Riding Hood loved talking to people, and as she was walking along the path, she met a wolf.

"Good morning, Little Girl, where are you off to in your beautiful red cloak?" said the wolf with a wicked smile.

Little Red Riding Hood put down her basket and said, "I'm taking some cakes to my grandmother, who's not very well."

"Where does your grandmother live?" asked the wolf.

"In the cottage at the end of this path," said Little Red Riding Hood.

Now the wolf was really very hungry and he wanted to eat up Little Red Riding Hood then and there. But he heard a woodcutter not far away and he ran off.

He went straight to the grandmother's cottage, where he found the old woman sitting up in bed. Before she knew what was happening, he ate her up in one gulp.

Then he put on the grandmother's nightdress and her nightcap, and climbed into her bed. He snuggled well down under the bedclothes and tried to hide himself.

Before long, Little Red Riding Hood came to the door with her basket of cakes and knocked.

"Come in," said the wolf, trying to make his voice sound soft.

At first, when she went in, Little Red Riding Hood thought that her grandmother must have a bad cold.

She went over to the bed. "What big eyes you have, Grandmama," she said as the wolf peered at her from under the nightcap.

"All the better to see you with, my dear," said the wolf.

"What big ears you have, Grandmama."

"All the better to hear you with, my dear," answered the wolf.

Then Little Red Riding Hood saw a long nose and a wide-open mouth. She wanted to scream but she said, very bravely, "What a big mouth you have, Grandmama."

At this the wolf opened his jaws wide.

"All the better to eat you with!"

he cried. And he jumped out of bed and ate up Little Red Riding Hood.

Just at that moment the woodcutter passed by the cottage. Noticing that the door was open, he went inside. When he saw the wolf, he quickly swung his ax and chopped off his head.

Little Red Riding Hood and then her grandmother stepped out, none the worse for their adventure.

Little Red Riding Hood thanked the woodcutter and ran home to tell her mother all that had happened. And after that day, she never, ever spoke to strangers.

THE TURNIP

~

ONCE THERE WAS A MAN who lived with his wife and little boy in a cottage in the country. One morning in May the man planted some turnip seeds.

Before long, little turnip leaves began to poke up through the brown earth. Then an odd thing happened. One turnip plant began to grow faster than all the rest. It grew and it grew and it grew.

"We must have that turnip for supper tonight," said the man.

So he tried to pull the big turnip out of the ground. He pulled and he pulled and he pulled. But the turnip stuck fast.

"Wife, wife," he called, "come and help me pull this great turnip."

His wife came running. Then she pulled the man, and the man pulled the turnip. Oh, how hard they pulled! But the turnip stuck fast.

"Son, son," called his mother, "come and help us pull this big turnip out of the ground."

The little boy came running and took tight hold of his mother. Then the boy pulled his mother, his mother pulled his father, and his father pulled the turnip. But still it stuck fast.

Then the little boy whistled for his dog.

"Come and help us," the boy said.

So the dog pulled the boy, the boy pulled his mother, his mother pulled his father, and his father pulled the turnip. But still it stuck fast.

Then the dog barked for the hen.

The hen came flying and grabbed tight hold of the dog's tail. Then she pulled the dog, the dog pulled the boy, the boy pulled his mother, his mother pulled his father, and his father pulled the turnip. But still the turnip stuck fast.

"Cluck, cluck, cluck!" cried the hen.

And the cock came flying to help. Then the cock pulled the hen, the hen pulled the dog, the dog pulled the boy, the boy pulled his mother, his mother pulled his father, his father pulled the turnip and...

Whooooosh!

Up came the turnip out of the ground, and down, backwards, they all tumbled in a heap. But they weren't hurt a bit and just got up laughing.

Then they rolled the turnip into the house and the boy's mother cooked it for their supper. Everyone had all they could eat and still there was enough left over for the next day, and the next, and the day after that!

THE LITTLE RED HEN

~

ONCE THERE WAS A PRETTY, neat little house. Inside it lived a Rooster, a Mouse and a Little Red Hen.

On another hill, not far away, was a very different little house. It had a door that wouldn't shut, windows that were dirty and broken, and paint that was peeling off. In this house lived a bad old mother Fox and her fierce young son.

One morning the mother Fox said, "On the hill over there you can see the house where the Rooster, the

Mouse and the Little Red Hen live. You and I haven't had very much to eat for a long time, and everyone in that house is very well fed and plump. They would make us a delicious dinner!"

The fierce young Fox was very hungry, so he got up at once and said, "I'll just find a sack. If you will get the big pot boiling, I'll go to that house on the hill and we'll have that Rooster, that Mouse and that Little Red Hen for our dinner!"

Now, on the very same morning, the Little Red Hen got up early, as she always did, and went downstairs to get the breakfast. The Rooster and the Mouse, who were lazy, did not come downstairs for some time.

"Who will get some sticks to light the fire?" asked the Little Red Hen.

"I won't," said the Rooster.

"I won't," said the Mouse.

"Then I'll have to do it myself," said the Little Red Hen. So off she ran to get the sticks.

When she had the fire burning, she said, "Who will go and get the kettle filled with water from the spring?"

"I won't," said the Rooster again.

"I won't," said the Mouse again.

"Then I'll have to do it myself," said the Little Red Hen, and off she ran to fill up the kettle.

While they were waiting for their breakfast, the Rooster and the Mouse curled up in comfortable armchairs. Soon they were asleep again.

It was just at this time that the fierce young Fox came up the hill with his sack and peeped in at the window. He stepped back and knocked loudly at the door.

"Who can that be?" said the Mouse, half opening his eyes.

"Go and find out, if you want to know," said the Rooster crossly.

"Perhaps it's the postman," said the Mouse to himself. So, without waiting to ask who it was, he lifted the latch and opened the door.

In rushed the big fierce Fox!

"Cock-a-doodle-do!" screamed the Rooster

as he jumped onto the back of the armchair.

"Oh! Oh! Oh!" squeaked the Mouse as he tried to run up the chimney.

But the Fox only laughed. He grabbed the Mouse by the tail and popped him into the sack. Then he caught the Rooster and pushed him in the sack too.

Just at that moment, in came the Little Red Hen, carrying the heavy kettle of water from the spring. Before she knew what was happening, the Fox quickly snatched her up and put her into the sack with the others. Then he tied a string tightly around the opening. And, with the sack over his shoulder, he set off down the hill.

The Rooster, the Mouse and the Little Red Hen were bumped together uncomfortably inside the sack.

The Rooster said, "Oh, I wish I hadn't been so cross!"

And the Mouse said, "Oh, I wish I hadn't been so lazy!"

But the Little Red Hen said, "It's never too late to try again."

As the Fox trudged along with his heavy load, the sun grew very hot. Soon he put the sack on the ground and sat down to rest. Before long he was fast asleep. Then

"Gr--umph...gr--mph,"

he began to snore. The noise was so loud that the Little Red Hen could hear him through the sack.

At once she took her scissors out of her apron pocket and cut a neat hole in the sack. Then out jumped: first the Mouse, then the Rooster, and last, the Little Red Hen.

"Quick! Quick!" she whispered. "Who will come and help me get some stones?"

"I will," said the Rooster.

"I will," said the Mouse.

"And I will," said the Little Red Hen.

Off they went together and each one brought back as big a rock as he could carry and put it into the sack. Then the Little Red Hen, who had a needle and thread in her pocket too, sewed up the hole very neatly.

When she had finished, the Little Red Hen, the Rooster and the Mouse ran off home as fast as they could go. Once inside, they bolted the door and then helped each other to get the best breakfast they had ever had!

After some time, the Fox woke up. He lifted the sack onto his back and went slowly up the hill to his house.

He called out, "Mother! Guess what I've got in my sack!"

"Is it – can it be – the Little Red Hen?"

"It is – and the Rooster – and the Mouse as well. They're very plump and heavy so they'll make us a splendid dinner."

His mother had the water all ready, boiling furiously in a pot over the fire. The Fox undid the string and emptied the sack straight into the pot.

Splash! Splash! Splash!

In went the three heavy rocks and out came the boiling hot water, all over the fierce young Fox and his bad old mother. Oh, how sore and burned and angry they were!

Never again did those wicked Foxes trouble the Rooster, the Mouse and the Little Red Hen, who always kept their door locked and lived happily ever after.

THE THREE BILLY GOATS GRUFF

O NCE UPON A TIME there were three Billy Goats. Their names were Big Billy Goat Gruff, Little Billy Goat Gruff and Baby Billy Goat Gruff.

They had lived all winter on a rocky hillside where no grass or flowers grew for them to eat. By the time spring came and the weather began to get warmer, they were thin and very hungry.

But over the bridge on the other side of the river, the hillside wasn't rocky at all. There the grass was thick and green with delicious flowers growing in it.

"We must cross the bridge to the other side, where we can find plenty to eat," said Big Billy Goat Gruff.

"But the wicked Troll who lives under the bridge won't let anyone cross," said Baby Billy Goat Gruff.

The Billy Goats Gruff were afraid to cross the bridge, but it was the only way to reach the lovely grass. They grew hungrier and hungrier every day until one day they put their heads together and made a plan.

First Baby Billy Goat Gruff went down the hillside and started across the bridge.

"Who goes there?" cried the Troll.

"It's only me, Baby Billy Goat Gruff."

"I'll eat you up," screamed the Troll. "I eat anyone who dares to cross my bridge."

"But I'm so small I'm only a mouthful," said the littlest Billy Goat Gruff. "If you wait for my bigger brother, he'll be along in a few minutes."

"Oh, all right," said the Troll crossly. So Baby Billy Goat Gruff went safely over the bridge.

Before long the next brother, Little Billy Goat Gruff, came to the bridge.

At once the Troll roared, "You can't cross my bridge. I'm going to eat you up!"

Little Billy Goat Gruff leaned over the side and called down to him, "I'm only a bit bigger than my baby brother and scarcely more than two mouthfuls. Wait for my big brother, who will be coming along soon."

"Oh, very well then," said the Troll, "but I'm getting very hungry and I won't wait much longer."

Before the old Troll could change his mind, Little Billy Goat Gruff was across the bridge and away up the hill to join his brother.

It wasn't long before Big Billy Goat Gruff came down the hill and started to cross the bridge. At once the Troll jumped out from underneath and reached up to catch him. But Big Billy Goat Gruff was very strong and he butted the Troll hard with his great horns. He tossed him high in the air and then . . . splash! . . . down . . . down he went, right into the middle of the river.

How Big Billy Goat Gruff laughed as he dashed across the bridge and up the hillside to join his two brothers.

Henny-Penny

~

ONE DAY WHEN Henny-Penny was scratching about for corn in the farmyard, an acorn fell down from the oak tree and hit her on the head.

"Goodness gracious," she cried, "the sky is falling. I must go and tell the king."

So off she went in a great hurry and soon she met Cocky-Locky. "Where are you going?" asked Cocky-Locky.

"I'm going to tell the king the sky is falling," said Henny-Penny.

"Can I come, too?" asked Cocky-Locky.

"Yes, do," said Henny-Penny.

So off went Henny-Penny and Cocky-Locky to tell the king the sky was falling and, before long, they met Ducky-Daddles.

"Where are you going?" asked Ducky-Daddles.

"Oh, we're going to tell the king the sky is falling," said Henny-Penny and Cocky-Locky.

"Can I come, too?" asked Ducky-Daddles.

"Yes, do," said Henny-Penny and Cocky-Locky.

So off went Henny-Penny, Cocky-Locky and Ducky-Daddles to tell the king the sky was falling and, before long, they met Goosey-Poosey.

"Where are you going?" asked Goosey-Poosey.

"Oh, we're going to tell the king the sky is falling," said Henny-Penny, Cocky-Locky and Ducky-Daddles.

"Can I come, too?" asked Goosey-Poosey.

"Yes, do," said Henny-Penny, Cocky-Locky and Ducky-Daddles.

So off went Henny-Penny, Cocky-Locky, Ducky-Daddles and Goosey-Poosey to tell the king the sky was falling and, before long, they met Turkey-Lurkey.

"Where are you going?" asked Turkey-Lurkey.

"Oh, we're going to tell the king the sky is falling," said Henny-Penny, Cocky-Locky, Ducky-Daddles and Goosey-Poosey.

"Can I come, too?" asked Turkey-Lurkey.

"Yes, do," said Henny-Penny, Cocky-Locky, Ducky-Daddles and Goosey-Poosey.

So off went Henny-Penny, Cocky-Locky, Ducky-Daddles, Goosey-Poosey and Turkey-Lurkey to tell the king the sky was falling.

They went along together – Henny-Penny, Cocky-Locky, Ducky-Daddles, Goosey-Poosey and Turkey-Lurkey – along and along, until they met Foxy-Woxy.

"Where are you going?" asked Foxy-Woxy.

"Oh, we're going to tell the king the sky is falling," said Henny-Penny, Cocky-Locky, Ducky-Daddles, Goosey-Poosey and Turkey-Lurkey.

"But you're not going the right way," said Foxy-Woxy. "I know the right way. Let me show you."

"Thank you," said Henny-Penny, Cocky-Locky, Ducky-Daddles, Goosey-Poosey and Turkey-Lurkey.

So off they all went with Foxy-Woxy leading the

way and, before long, they came to a dark hole. Now this was really the home of Foxy-Woxy, but he said, "This is the shortest way to the king's palace. Follow me."

So Foxy-Woxy went a little way down the hole and waited for Henny-Penny, Cocky-Locky, Ducky-Daddles, Goosey-Poosey and Turkey-Lurkey.

First came Turkey-Lurkey.

"Snap!" Foxy-Woxy bit off Turkey-Lurkey's head.

Next came Goosey-Poosey.

"Snap!" Foxy-Woxy bit off Goosey-Poosey's head.

Next came Ducky-Daddles.

"Snap!" Foxy-Woxy bit off Ducky-Daddles's head.

Next came Cocky-Locky.

"Snap!" But this time Foxy-Woxy was getting tired and he missed, so that Cocky-Locky managed to call out to Henny-Penny, "Look out! Don't come!"

Henny-Penny heard Cocky-Locky and ran back home to the farmyard as fast as she could go. And that was why she never told the king the sky was falling.

GOLDILOCKS AND THE THREE BEARS
~

ONCE UPON A TIME, there were three bears who
lived together in their own little house in the
woods. There was a great big father bear, a middle-sized
mother bear and a little baby bear. They each had a
special bowl for porridge, a special chair for sitting in,
and a special bed to sleep in.

One morning the mother bear made their porridge
for breakfast and poured it out into the great big bowl,
the middle-sized bowl and the little baby bowl. But it

was so hot the bears decided to go for a walk while
it cooled.

Now a little girl called Goldilocks was walking in
the woods that morning and she came across the bears'
house. She knocked on the door, and when there was
no reply, she crept slowly in.

"Oh! Oh!" she cried when she saw the bowls of
porridge. "I'm so hungry, I must have just one
spoonful."

First she went to the great big bowl and took a
taste. "Too hot!" she said.

Then she went to the middle-sized bowl and tried
that porridge. "Too cold," she said.

Last she went to the little baby bowl. "Oh! Oh!
Just right!" she cried, and she ate it all up, every bit.

Then Goldilocks saw the great big chair and climbed
into it. "Too big," she said, and climbed down quickly.

Next she went to the middle-sized chair and sat
down. "Too hard," she said.

Then she went quickly to the little baby chair.
"It just fits," she said happily. But really the chair
was too small for her and – CRACK – it broke,

and down she tumbled.

Then she went into the next room, where she saw three neat beds. First she climbed into the great big bed, but it was too high.

Next she climbed into the middle-sized bed, but it was too low.

Then she saw the little baby bed. "Oh! Oh!" she cried. "This is just right." She got in, pulled up the covers, and went fast asleep.

Before long the three bears came home for their breakfast. First the great big bear went to eat his porridge. He took one look and said in his great rough voice, "Somebody has been eating my porridge!"

Then the middle-sized bear looked into her bowl and said in her middle-sized voice, "And somebody has been eating my porridge, too!"

Finally the little baby bear went to his bowl. "Oh! Oh!" he cried in his little baby voice. "Somebody's been eating my porridge and has eaten it all up!"

After that, all three bears wanted to sit down. The great big bear went to his great big chair and saw that the cushion had been squashed down.

"Somebody has been sitting in my chair,"

he cried in his great big voice.

Then the middle-sized mother bear went to her middle-sized chair and found her cushion on the floor.

"Somebody has been sitting in my chair,"

she said in her middle-sized voice.

Then the little baby bear hurried to his chair. "Oh! Oh!" he cried in his little baby voice.

"Somebody has been sitting
in my chair and broken it all to bits!"

The three bears, feeling very sad, went into the bedroom.

First the great big bear looked at his bed.

"Somebody has been lying in my bed,"

he said in his great big voice.

Then the middle-sized bear saw her bed all rumpled up and she cried in her middle-sized voice,

"Oh dear, somebody has been
lying in my bed."

By this time the little baby bear had gone to his little baby bed and he cried,

"Somebody has been lying in my bed
and she's still here!"

This time his little baby voice was so high and squeaky that Goldilocks woke up with a start and sat up. There on one side of the bed were the three bears, all looking down at her.

Now Goldilocks did not know that they were kind bears and she was very frightened. She screamed, jumped out of the bed, ran to the open window and quickly climbed out. Then she ran home to her mother as fast as she possibly could.

As for the bears, they put things to rights, and since
Goldilocks never came again, they lived happily ever after.

THE THREE LITTLE PIGS

O NCE THERE WERE three little pigs who grew up and left their mother to find homes for themselves. The first little pig set out, and before long he met a man with a bundle of straw.

"Please, Man," said the pig, "will you let me have that bundle of straw to build my house?"

"Yes, here, take it," said the kind man. The little pig was very pleased and at once built himself a house of straw.

He had hardly moved in when a wolf came walking by and, seeing the new house, knocked on the door.

"Little pig, little pig," he said, "open up the door and let me in."

Now the little pig's mother had warned him about strangers, so he said, "No, not by the hair of my chinny-chin-chin, I'll not let you in."

"Then I'll huff and I'll puff and I'll blow your house down!" cried the wolf.

But the little pig went on saying, "No, not by the hair of my chinny-chin-chin, I'll not let you in."

So the old wolf huffed and he puffed and he blew the house down, and ate up the little pig.

The second little pig said good-bye to his mother and set out. Before long he met a man with a bundle of sticks.

"Please, Man," he said, "will you let me have that bundle of sticks to build my house?"

"Yes, you can have it. Here it is," said the kind man.

So the second little pig was very pleased and used the sticks to build himself a house. He had hardly moved in when the wolf came walking by and knocked on the door.

"Little pig, little pig," he said, "open up your door and let me in."

Now the second little pig remembered what his mother had told him, so he, too, said, "No, not by the hair of my chinny-chin-chin, I'll not let you in."

"Then I'll huff and I'll puff and I'll blow your house down!" cried the wolf.

But the little pig went on saying, "No, not by the hair of my chinny-chin-chin, I'll not let you in!"

So again, the old wolf huffed and he puffed, and he

huffed and he puffed. This time it was much harder work but, finally, down came the house and he ate up the second little pig.

Then, last of all, the third little pig set out and met a man with a load of bricks.

"Please, Man," he said, "will you let me have that load of bricks to build my house?"

"Yes, here they are – all for you," said the kind man. The third little pig was very pleased, and built himself a brick house.

Again the wolf came along, and again he said, "Little pig, little pig, open your door and let me in."

But, like his brothers, the third little pig said, "No, not by the hair of my chinny-chin-chin, I'll not let you in."

"Then I'll huff and I'll puff and I'll blow your house down!" cried the wolf.

And when the third little pig wouldn't open the door, he huffed and he puffed, and he huffed and he puffed. Then he tried again, but the brick house was so strong that he could not blow it down.

This made the wolf so angry that he jumped onto the roof of the little brick house and roared down the chimney, "I'm coming down to eat you up!"

The little pig had put a pot full of boiling water on the fire and now he took off the lid. Down the chimney tumbled the wolf and –

SPLASH!

– he fell right into the pot.

Quickly the little pig banged on the cover and boiled up the old wolf for his dinner.

And so the clever little pig lived happily ever after.

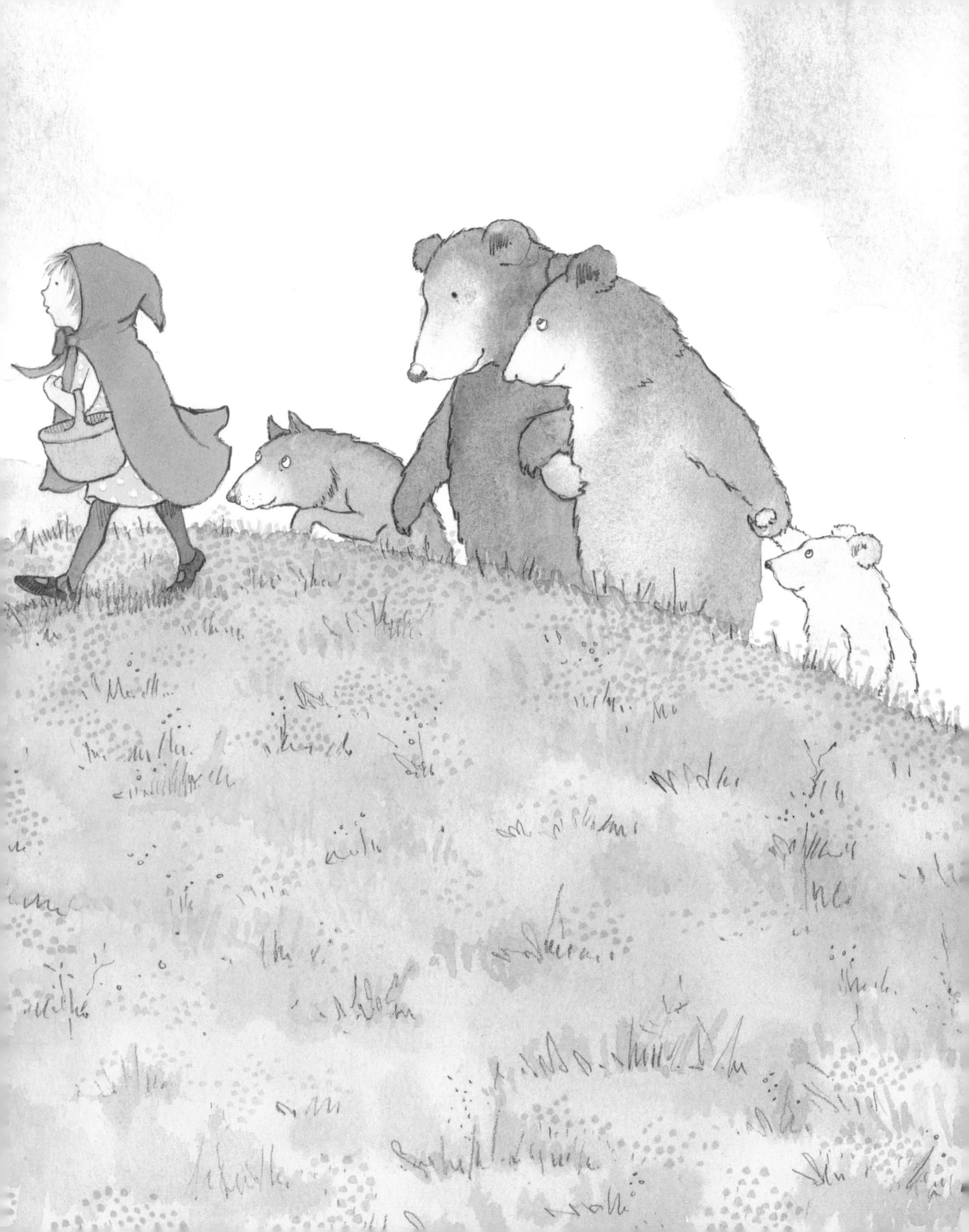